Making Their Mark: Women In Sports™

Bonnie Blair
Speed Skater

Liza N. Burby

The Rosen Publishing Group's
PowerKids Press™
New York

Published in 1997 by The Rosen Publishing Group, Inc.
29 East 21st Street, New York, NY 10010

First Edition

Book Design: Erin McKenna

Photo Credits: Cover and pp. 4, 15, 16, 19, 20 © AP/Wide World Photos, Inc; p. 7 © John Terence Turner/FPG International Corp.; pp. 8, 11,12 © Thomas Zimmermann/FPG International Corp.

Burby, Liza N.
    Bonnie Blair / by Liza N. Burby
         p.   cm. — (Making their mark: women in sports)
    Includes index.
    Summary: Covers the life and achievements of the Olympic speed skater Bonnie Blair.
    ISBN 0-8239-5066-2 (lib. bdg.)
    1. Blair, Bonnie, 1964– —Juvenile literature. 2. Women speed skaters—United States—Biography—Juvenile literature. [1. Blair, Bonnie, 1964– . 2. Ice Skaters. 3. Women—Biography.] I. Title. II. Series: Burby, Liza N. Making their mark.
GV850.B63B87 1997
796.91'4'092—dc21
[B]   96–53333
                                                                                          CIP
                                                                                          AC

Manufactured in the United States of America

Contents

Born to Skate

There was never any doubt that Bonnie Blair would be an ice skater. She was born into a **speed skating** (SPEED SKAY-ting) family on March 18, 1964, in Cornwall, New York. That day, three of her five brothers and sisters were in a race. Bonnie's father was with them. They all heard that a new Blair speed skater had been born. No one knew then just how fast that speed skater would one day be.

◄ Bonnie believes in working as hard as you can to be the best you can be.

5

First Time on the Ice

When Bonnie was a baby, the Blair family moved to Champaign, Illinois. It was so cold there that they were able to skate on frozen ponds and **rinks** (RINKS) year-round. Bonnie was just two years old when her brothers and sisters decided that she should learn to ice skate. They put skates over her little shoes and put her on the ice. Bonnie loved it. Soon she was skating as well as she walked. What she liked best was to skate fast.

Like this little boy, Bonnie learned to skate at an early age. ▶

A Racing Family

Every winter weekend, the Blairs would travel to a different **meet** (MEET). Bonnie's parents liked to watch their children **compete** (kum-PEET) in races. But they also taught their children that it didn't matter if they won as long as they did their best. Often Bonnie would take naps between the races. She skated her first race when she was only four years old. By the time she was six, she was winning races against girls who were three years older than she was.

◀ During the winter, Bonnie spent every weekend at skating meets, competing in races.

Early Lessons

When she was seven, Bonnie raced in the Illinois Championships. She learned a lot about ice racing. She was a **pack racer** (PAK RAY-ser). That meant she raced against lots of other skaters. She learned that if she didn't start her race very fast, she would lose. She was a small girl, but that didn't bother her. She learned how to skate around the bigger kids without getting knocked down. She also learned how to work hard enough to become a winner.

Pack racing can be difficult because you are skating very close to other skaters. ▶

A New Style

Bonnie was one of the fastest girl skaters in the country. She was only twelve when her father said that someday she would win an Olympic gold medal. From then on she knew she wanted to work to make that happen. She learned how to skate Olympic-style. This meant that she wouldn't be racing against other skaters. Instead, she raced against a clock to get the fastest time. It didn't take long before she was winning these races, too.

◀ In Olympic-style skating, a skater races against a clock instead of against other skaters.

Training for the Olympics

Bonnie worked hard for the 1984 Olympics in Sarajevo, Yugoslavia. She bicycled. She ran. She lifted weights. She was the only girl at her high school who exercised with the boys' football team. But Bonnie's family did not have enough money to pay for coaches and for Bonnie to travel to races. It looked as if she may not be able to go to the Olympics after all. But the Champaign police department collected money for Bonnie. She was on her way to Sarajevo!

Love and support from Bonnie's friends and family helped her get ahead in speed skating. ▶

A Top Winner

In the 1984 Olympics, Bonnie skated as fast as she could. She came in eighth place, but she wasn't unhappy. She decided that she would work even harder for the next Olympics and win the gold medal. In 1985, she won five first-place awards at the National Sports Festival. That was more wins than anyone else that year. She even won one of the awards by skating on the men's team!

◀ Bonnie swings her arms when she skates to help her go faster.

A Gold Medal at Last

Life magazine called Bonnie the "best bet for gold" in 1988. The United States hoped that she would win a medal at the Winter Olympics in Calgary, Canada. She did better than that. She won the gold medal she had dreamed about. She also won a bronze medal. She was the only American athlete to win two medals that year. At the 1992 Olympics in Albertville, France, she won two medals again. This time both of her medals were gold. She was called the best **amateur** (AM-ah-cher) athlete in the country.

Bonnie's gold medal made ▶
Americans proud.

America's Shining Star

Bonnie was almost 30 at the 1994 Olympic Games in Lillehammer, Norway. That is old for a woman speed skater. She decided that the 1994 Games would be her last. Bonnie won two more Olympic gold medals that year. In her **career** (kah-REER) as a speed skater, she had won five gold medals. This is more than any other woman athlete in history. She is one of America's shining stars.

Bonnie is the only American woman to win gold medals at three Olympics in a row.

A Girl Who Likes to Skate Fast

Bonnie is still the fastest woman speed skater in the world. With hard work and **determination** (dee-TER-min-AY-shun), she made her dream of winning a gold medal come true. But even after all her medals, she says that what is more important to her than winning is knowing she has done her best. She says she is still just a girl who likes to skate fast.

Glossary

amateur (AM-ah-cher) Someone who plays a sport but does not get paid for it.

career (kah-REER) The work a person chooses to do.

compete (kum-PEET) To try to win something.

determination (dee-TER-min-AY-shun) Wanting to do something no matter how hard a person has to work.

meet (MEET) A race.

pack racer (PAK RAY-ser) An ice skater who races against a lot of skaters at once.

rink (RINK) An indoor area for ice skating.

speed skating (SPEED SKAY-ting) When people race as fast as they can on ice skates.

23

Index